Note to parents, carers and teachers

Read it yourself is a series of modern stories, favourite characters and traditional tales written in a simple way for children who are learning to read. The books can be read independently or as part of a guided reading session.

Each book is carefully structured to include many high-frequency words vital for first reading. The sentences on each page are supported closely by pictures to help with understanding, and to offer lively details to talk about.

The books are graded into four levels that progressively introduce wider vocabulary and longer stories as a reader's ability and confidence grows.

Ideas for use

- Begin by looking through the book and talking about the pictures. Has your child heard this story before?

- Help your child with any words he does not know, either by helping him to sound them out or supplying them yourself.

- Developing readers can be concentrating so hard on the words that they sometimes don't fully grasp the meaning of what they're reading. Answering the puzzle questions on pages 30 and 31 will help with understanding.

For more information and advice on Read it yourself and book banding, visit **www.ladybird.com/readityourself**

Book Band 4

Level 1 is ideal for children who have received some initial reading instruction. Each story is told very simply, using a small number of frequently repeated words.

Special features:

The old woman

The mother

The little girl

The magic porridge pot

6

7

Opening pages introduce key story words

Careful match between story and pictures

Large, clear type

Once upon a time, a little girl met an old woman.

The old woman gave her a magic porridge pot.

8

9

Educational Consultant: Geraldine Taylor
Book Banding Consultant: Kate Ruttle

A catalogue record for this book is available from the British Library

Published by Ladybird Books Ltd
80 Strand, London, WC2R 0RL
A Penguin Company

003

ISBN: 978-0-72327-272-4

Printed in China

The Magic Porridge Pot

Illustrated by Laura Barella

The old woman

The little girl

The mother

The magic porridge pot

Once upon a time,
a little girl met an
old woman.

The old woman gave her
a magic porridge pot.

"Cook, little pot, cook,"
said the old woman.

And the little pot
cooked some porridge.

"Stop, little pot, stop,"
said the old woman.

And the little pot
stopped cooking.

The little girl took the
magic porridge pot
to her mother.

"Cook, little pot, cook,"
said the little girl's mother.

And the little pot cooked
some porridge.

Soon the kitchen
was full of porridge.

And still the magic
porridge pot went
on cooking.

Soon the house was
full of porridge.

And still the magic
porridge pot went
on cooking.

Soon the street
was full of porridge.

And still the magic
porridge pot went
on cooking.

Soon the whole town
was full of porridge.

And still the magic
porridge pot went
on cooking.

"Stop, little pot, stop!"
said the little girl.

At last the magic
porridge pot
stopped cooking.

But the whole town is still eating porridge!

How much do you remember about the story of The Magic Porridge Pot? Answer these questions and find out!

- Who gives the magic porridge pot to the little girl?

- What does the old woman say to make the pot start cooking?

- What does the little girl say to make the pot stop cooking?

Look at the pictures from the story and say the order they should go in.

A

B

C

D

Read it yourself with Ladybird

Tick the books you've read!

For children who are ready to take their first steps in reading.

Level 1

- The Enormous Turnip ☐
- Fairy Friends ☐
- Goldilocks and the Three Bears ☐
- Little Red Hen ☐
- The Magic Porridge Pot ☐
- Little Creatures ☐
- Recycling Fun! ☐
- The Princess and the Pea ☐
- Cinderella ☐
- Rex the Big Dinosaur ☐
- The Tale of Peter Rabbit ☐
- The Three Billy Goats Gruff ☐
- Why Giraffe has a Long Neck ☐
- Topsy and Tim Go to the Zoo ☐
- The Ugly Duckling ☐
- The Emperor's New Clothes ☐

For beginner readers who can read short, simple sentences with help.

Level 2

- Beauty and the Beast ☐
- Chicken Licken ☐
- Little Red Riding Hood ☐
- Nature Trail ☐
- Sports Day ☐
- Pirate School ☐
- Rumpelstiltskin ☐
- Sleeping Beauty ☐
- The Gingerbread Man ☐
- Sly Fox and Red Hen ☐
- The Tale of Jemima Puddle-Duck ☐
- The Three Little Pigs ☐
- Why Lion Roarrrs! ☐
- Topsy and Tim The Big Race ☐
- Town Mouse and Country Mouse ☐
- Dom's Dragon ☐

Available on the App Store

The Read it yourself with Ladybird app is now available for iPad, iPhone and iPod touch

App also available on Android devices